The Adventures of SPARKY

The Adventures of SPARKY,
the Elephant from Tipton, and His Wonderful Friends

Written by Philip Mousley
Illustrations by Omar Aranda

The Adventures of Sparky, the Elephant from Tipton, and His Wonderful Friends
Philip Mousley

Published by Aspect Design, 2019

Printed and bound by Aspect Design
89 Newtown Road, Malvern, Worcs. WR14 1PD
United Kingdom
Tel: 01684 561567
E-mail: allan@aspect-design.net
Website: www.aspect-design.net

Illustrations Copyright © 2019 Omar Aranda
Cover design Copyright © 2019 Niki Merrett

ISBN 978-1-912078-84-4

It was the last day of Stacy's safari holiday in Africa. She was travelling across the hot dusty plains when she spotted a very small elephant in some bushes. She asked her driver to stop the car and went to have a closer look.

The baby elephant had become separated from his herd and was all alone. She gave him a drink and something to eat from her rucksack and he trumpeted his thanks. Looking at him, she knew she couldn't leave him there. She had to take him home and look after him because he was so lost!

Stacy became the elephant's foster mother. She called him Sparky because he was always full of fun and mischief.

Back in Tipton where she lived, Stacy gave Sparky a room of his own.

"The West Midlands are a bit different from Central Africa," she told him. "We don't want you getting homesick now, do we?"

So she filled the room with things that reminded him of home. There were photographs of different animals all over the walls - especially elephants enjoying themselves in the sunshine and throwing water over each other to keep cool.

Although Stacy did everything she could to make him happy, Sparky soon began to feel lonely. He missed Africa and wanted to go back there as soon as he could, but he knew it was a very long way to get there.

When he was a bit older, Sparky went to Dudley Zoo so he could be with the other elephants and animals from his homeland. Sometimes he was allowed to stay the night at the zoo. That was fun . . . but scary!

"I d-d-don't like all the rustling noises!" the baby elephant whispered.

"Come and hide behind me," said Lukey, the biggest elephant at the zoo.

Lukey and the other elephants made sure Sparky was kept safe. In the winter, they gave him a woolly hat and scarf to wear when it was cold. It was cold quite a lot in Dudley at night!

Sparky's zoo friends knew he longed to go home and find his real family. He wanted to live with his proper mother and all his brothers, sisters, uncles, aunts and cousins that made up the herd in Africa.

"You're not big enough to travel yet," said Lukey wisely. "Stay here and have some fun until you're ready to go."

Sparky was given a little bike that he loved to ride. Lots of people paid money to watch him pedalling round and round in circles and doing tricks like steering with his trunk. He felt really happy when the visitors clapped and cheered him.

Amber and Bella, his young lady friends at the zoo, liked to join in the show. They dressed up and tried out their new dance routines which delighted the crowd even more.

"I do love living here," Sparky said to himself, "but it's time to move on."

Sparky's best friend was a Giant Toad called

Frank who lived in the Reptile House at Dudley Zoo. He would sneak into the elephant enclosure as often as he could so the two of them could lark about together. Frank was keen to see other people and places around the world.

"I'm coming with you," he said.

So the following Monday they set off early, heading for the seaside where they hoped to buy a couple of tickets for a ship heading for Africa. Sparky's shows had made a lot of money and he'd been given some to keep for himself.

Sparky was riding his bike. Frank travelled in the basket at the front because he jumped around a lot when he got excited and that was dangerous and caused trouble. The basket was full of sandwiches, sausage rolls and a fruit cake with icing (Sparky's favourite) that Lukey's wife, Molly, had given them for the journey.

"Please sit still, Frank, you're squashing everything," Sparky begged.

"I'm trying, I'm trying!" Frank replied. "But it's not easy, you know!"

So they had to stop to eat all the food and, after a long day's pedalling, they eventually reached the seaside.

Frank spotted some ships in the harbour.

"Excuse me, sir," he said to a captain called Ray in his politest croak. "Where are you going?"

"Casablanca," Ray replied. "That's a port on the coast of Africa."

"Please may we come with you?" asked Sparky.

Captain Ray liked elephants and toads and gave them a very nice cabin for the trip.

When the ship docked in Casablanca, they said goodbye to their friend and headed straight for the railway station. Ray had told them they needed to travel to a place called Marrakesh from where they could travel to Sparky's homeland.

The train was hot and dusty and the seats were not very comfortable, but at last they reached their destination. They felt hungry and thirsty.

"Let's go to the market," suggested Sparky.

The market was noisy and crowded. They walked around, eating and drinking, gazing in awe at the brightly coloured clothes, carpets and jewellery on sale at the stalls.

There was also a snake-charmer who was playing a flute and trying to get his snake to do a little dance.

"I am not dancing today," shouted the snake. "I'm a very important person. This is beneath my dignity!"

"I recognise that voice!" Frank gasped.

They hurried over and found Rupert, a snake who had once lived in the Reptile House at Dudley Zoo.

"What are you guys doing here?" he asked in amazement.

"Travelling back to my family," explained Sparky.

"Can I come?" cried Rupert, slithering out of his basket.

Now there were three of them heading south to the heart of Africa.

To reach Sparky's family, the travellers had to cross the Sahara Desert. This is the biggest desert in the world, thousands of miles of burning sand stretching in all directions. They knew it would be a long and difficult journey, so they bought all the things they needed including lots and lots of water and some Factor 50 sun cream. The days were boiling hot and the nights freezing cold as they made their way steadily across the empty wilderness.

On the ninth day, Frank croaked, "I need a drink."

"The water's all gone," said Sparky.

"What?" gasped Rupert. "We're not there yet!"

The friends were now in real trouble. Without water, they could not go on.

"I can see some!" Rupert cried, wriggling towards a beautiful blue pool surrounded by leafy palm trees. But it wasn't really there!

"It's just a mirage," Frank sighed. "You see things like that when you're really thirsty."

They staggered on with Sparky giving the other two a ride on his back.

"There's a river!" Frank whooped, pointing ahead.

"It's just another mirage," sighed Rupert.

"No, it's not!" laughed Sparky, breaking into a run. "I can see it too."

Soon they had drunk their fill and were splashing about in the cool flowing water.

Sparky's family lived near a small town called Loul in a country called Senegal. It would take several more days to get there, but they'd filled their water bottles at the river and there was food to be found on the way.

"Look at all these beautiful animals!" exclaimed Rupert.

A gazelle bounced past them, looking as if it had springs on its feet. Some wildebeest followed, travelling to another part of the country. And a hippo cooled himself in a muddy hollow.

"It's so beautiful here," Frank sighed.

That evening, as they lay on the ground gazing up at the stars, Sparky knew he would never return to Tipton. This made him sad because it meant he'd never see Stacy again, but here was where he belonged. This was home.

Next morning, when the three friends woke up, the wind was howling across the plain and a strange orange cloud came rolling towards them.

"What is it?" asked Frank.

"Never seen anything like it before in my life," said Sparky.

"I have!" gulped Rupert. "It's a dust storm. RUN!"

The billowing orange dust soon engulfed them as they fled in different directions, gasping and spluttering for air. None of them could see where they were going. Frank bumped into a big rock and knocked himself out, Rupert fell down a deep crack in the ground and Sparky just ran and ran as he tried to get away from the choking dust.

When the storm passed, the three friends were separated. Each one was alone in a strange land. They raced about, shouting and looking for each other, but they were too far apart to be found.

"Wish I'd never come here now," Sparky sobbed.

Three young lionesses called Amy, Hayle and Lottie were passing nearby. They heard Sparky crying and came to see what was wrong.

"I've lost my friends and I can't find my family," he wailed.

"We'll help you to find both," said Hayle.

Lottie set off in search of Frank. She soon found him sitting by a rock nursing a lump on his head and took him back to Sparky.

Meanwhile, Amy went looking for Rupert. She ran everywhere without finding him and lay down beside a crack in the ground for a rest. Next moment he slithered out of it and was soon reunited with Sparky too.

The lions led Sparky, Frank and Rupert towards the township of Loul. A girl called Marie came to meet them. She knew the lions well, having played with them when they were cubs.

"I'll take you to your family," she told Sparky.

Waving goodbye to their lion friends, they followed Marie as she walked round to the other side of town. Sparky felt his heart beating fast as they approached a watering-hole beside some trees. His Uncle Carl was tugging at a tree with his Cousin James. Standing in the water, with her back to him, was his mother Eleanor.

Sparky raced over and splashed into the water. "Hello, Mum!" he trumpeted. Eleanor could not believe her eyes. "I never thought I'd see you again!" she cried.

Then she covered her long-lost son in kisses and
hugged him until he could hardly breathe. "Don't you ever
go away again!" Eleanor scolded. "I won't" Sparky promised.

Sparky was taken to meet the members of his family. As well as being introduced to Carl and James, he met his baby brother Jimmy and his older brother Archie. They made him feel welcome straight away by squirting him with water and taking him for a roll in the mud.

They were practicing trumpeting to see who was the loudest when their mum arrived with a massive male elephant.

"Hi, Dad!" called Archie and Jimmy together.

"You're my father?" said Sparky, looking up curiously.

"I am indeed," chuckled the friendly giant. "Name's Alfie, but you must call me Dad too. I'm so glad you're safely home."

"So am I," said his son.

As Sparky settled in to his new life with his family, he felt guilty about Frank and Rupert. His friends had travelled so far with him and gone through so many hardships to get here, he felt he was ignoring them now. But he need not have worried.

Frank had taken up residence beside a small pond and was courting a nice lady Giant Toad called Tammy. He spent hours impressing her with his seeming endless dance moves – all hip-hop, of course.

Meanwhile, Rupert had made himself a home at some nice cool rocks where he spent his days snoozing in the shade underneath them and going out after dark for food.

Now everybody who knew Sparky was happy . . .

except one. Back in Tipton, Stacy felt very sad. Every time she looked into the elephant's room, with its pictures of Africa on the walls and ornaments on the bedside table, tears came into her eyes. Often she called in at Dudley Zoo to see if he'd been found or come back, but he was never there.

Then, one day, Molly overheard Stacy talking to a keeper. She remembered making the picnic for Sparky and his friends and hurried over to tell her.

"Did they say where they were going?" Stacy asked excitedly.

"Home," answered Molly. "Sparky said he was going home."

This was the news Sparky's foster-mum had been waiting for. She rushed to the bank and drew out her savings.

"I have enough for another safari holiday and to buy him a present," she chuckled on her way to the shops.

When everything was packed and ready, Stacy set off on her journey. She didn't need to travel by boat, train and on foot. She flew to Africa in a huge aeroplane and arrived later the very same day. She hired a jeep with a driver and headed for Loul.

"I just hope Sparky remembers me," she said to herself.

Sparky was playing ball with Jimmy, batting it

backwards and forwards with their trunks, when the jeep arrived. He heard someone calling his name and turned round to see a familiar figure racing towards him.

"Stacy!" he cried in delight.

Lots more hugging and kissing followed, watched by his real mother.

"Thank you for rescuing Sparky when he was lost," said Eleanor. "Who knows what could have happened to a tiny elephant all alone on the plains?"

Now everyone was happy. Stacy stayed with the elephant family for the whole of her holiday, joining in Sparky's games.

"But no way I'm rolling in the mud," she told him.

When Stacy went home, she left the present she'd brought Sparky as a surprise. His family gathered round eagerly as he tore the top off the big cardboard box with his trunk. Then he lifted out another little bike. It was brand new with bright blue paintwork and shiny chrome handlebars. Sparky jumped onto the saddle and peddled round in a circle. The others had never seen an elephant riding a bike before and all they trumpeted with laughter until they cried.

"Now I have everything," Sparky sighed joyfully.